This book belongs to an adventurer named

_____

The Adventures of Olive the Oligator

A Chilly Place!

By Zenny Roy & Illustrated by Ash Jackson

Edited by Caleb Burroughs and Kendall Royzen

ISBN 978-1-7923-0372-2 (Hardcover)

Published by Alex Royzen

Printed in China

For K, C, and A. My muses.

Way down deep in the Louisiana swamp lived an Oligator... wait... a WHAT?!?

An Oligator!

Well, her name was Olive and she was actually an alligator... But Olive called her alligator self an Oligator!

Olive was part of a **HUGE** Oligator family. She had her mama gator, her papa gator, and her 152 brother and sister gators.

In fact, they had so many gators in Olive's Oligator family that everyone had to wear a nametag just to keep all those Oligators straight!

Say cheese, Pete!

Show us those pointy pearly whites, Fran!

Look this way, Liam!

All of Olive's brothers and sisters loved that splishy, splashy, swampy stomping ground where the Oligator family had lived for years and years.

But Olive was different...she wanted to explore the whole wide world.

So, at Olive the Oligator's 10th birthday party, she bravely stood up and told her family she was going to leave the swamp and go on an adventure!

Her many, many brothers and sisters all stared at Olive... and burst out laughing.

"Where are you going to GO?"

"What will you DO there?"

"Will you live in another SWAMP?"

They couldn't understand why she would ever want to leave!

But that didn't stop Olive the Oligator!

NO WAY!

She packed up her suitcase, said goodbye to her mama gator, her papa gator, and her 152 brother and sister gators, and dove downstream heading south from her family's swampy home.

Olive swam and swam. She used her mighty Oligator tail to propel her through rough waters and tough currents.

Before she knew it, Olive was in the middle of a vast ocean with no land in sight from any direction!

Like any good Oligator, Olive had been taking swim lessons since the day she'd hatched, so she kept right on swimming without a care.

She knew she'd find an adventure soon...

At last, Olive saw someplace large and white that wasn't so distant... a new place to explore!

And a place that looked much different from home....

When Olive reached the large white someplace, she climbed up onto it.

BRRRRRRRR!!

It nearly **froze** her Oligator toes!

Instead of muddy water, leaves, and warm sunshine like her family swamp, there was white powder everywhere and more of it fell all over Olive's chilly Oligator snout!

Olive made her way over to a noise she heard and saw something slowly appear over the top of a big white hill.

shuffle, shuffle, shuffle

A small black and white creature was making its way towards her!

A little animal with a pointy orange beak wobbled towards Olive on his webbed feet, patting a plump white tummy with his black floppy flippers.

"What are YOU!?" asked Olive. She had never seen such a creature!

"What am I!? More like, what are YOU!?" the funny fellow responded. "I am a penguin and my name is Pierce."

"It's nice to eat... errrr... meet you Pierce!" Olive said. "My name is Olive and I'm an Oligator!"

"An Oligator...? I've never heard of those before... Anyhoo, welcome to Antarctica!" Pierce said jovially.

"Ant-where-tick-huh?" Olive tried to repeat the name without much success.

"ANT-ARC-TIC-A," sounded out Pierce. "It's full of icebergs, all the way at the bottom of the world, and the coldest place ever!"

The bottom of the world?! That meant Olive had swum across an entire ocean! She had traveled a long way from her swampy home.

She also realized how hungry the journey had made her...

Olive looked at Pierce and realized he looked mighty tasty. She opened her wide jaws and began to lean in towards him for a quick snack...

But before Olive could snag him, Pierce popped something that certainly wasn't a penguin into her hungry Oligator mouth!

Olive the Oligator tasted something... sweet... and creamy... and crunchy... a new and delicious combination of flavors she had never tasted before.

"What is this?!" A pleasantly surprised Olive gasped as she swallowed.

"You Oligators must live someplace really warm," said Pierce.

"I just gave you a bite of ice cream, one of the yummiest treats we have down here.

The cone is **crunchy**, the ice cream is **creamy**, and the toppings are **sweet!**

Ice cream makes EVERYTHING better."

Olive thought for a moment and felt...well... bad.

"Pierce, I'm sorry I let my Oligator instincts get ahead of me. That ice cream was pretty amazing... Maybe you can show me some more special stuff about Antarctica...?" Olive asked hopefully.

Pierce thought about it for a second. "Ok, Olive. I forgive you! I can show you all the fun things we do in the cold if you promise we'll be friends forever and keep an open mind!"

"DEAL!!" said Olive and sealed it by giving Pierce a warm Oligator hug.

First, Pierce taught Olive how to build a snow fort!

Then he showed her how to roll the snow in his flippers and pack it into round balls... and once they had a big pile of them all ready to go....

Pierce threw one at Olive and they had a snowball fight!

Pierce showed Olive how to belly slide off an iceberg into the frigid water!

While they were laughing and sliding, a group of friendly seals appeared and they all played a game of Marco Polo!

"MARCO!!!" Olive shouted.

"POLO!!!" Pierce and the seals yelled back.

They even went walrus tipping!

Olive would **never ever** have experienced any of this stuff in the Oligator swamp.

After their exhausting day of Antarctica activities, Pierce took Olive by her slick and scaly hand and waddled next to her as they headed over to his village.

He introduced her to his penguin friends and family and they all settled in for the night.

Olive had an amazing time visiting Antarctica, meeting Pierce the Penguin, and having lots of new... and cold... experiences.

She sent a postcard back to the Oligator swamp and began to think about where the next adventure would take her!